Rupert Builds A Nest

EGMONT

One sunny day, Rupert and Ping Pong set out to play in the forest.

But they were only half-way over the bridge when they heard a rumbling noise. They jumped apart only just in time for Freddy Fox to come hurtling through on his skateboard.

"Whee!" shouted Freddy. "We're the fastest flying foxes in the forest!"

3

A few seconds later, Freda Fox came whizzing past as well.

Poor little Ming had only just avoided being hit by Freddy. Now she fell forward onto her front paws.

"Oops, sorry!" the foxes called back as they zoomed into the distance.

Ping Pong and Rupert started playing tag in the forest.

Rupert suddenely stopped. Sitting on the ground ahead of them was a bird's nest.

"I don't think that's meant to be there!" he exclaimed.

Then they heard birdsong. A bird was hopping anxiously around in the tree overhead.

8

"**O**h dear!" worried Ping Pong. "The nest must have fallen out of the tree!"

"Can you do nest-building magic?" Rupert asked.

Ping Pong looked unsure. "I haven't learnt that yet. Maybe I could use . . ."

"Let's ask Raggety," Rupert interrupted. "He might know what to do."

Ping Pong looked upset.

Rupert called Raggety's name, but the little elf did not appear. Instead, the Fox Twins sidled into the clearing.

"Sorry about the nest . . ." Freddy mumbled.

"We were going really fast, and I bumped into the tree," Freda muttered. "And Freddy bumped into me, and the nest fell out."

Then Raggety came into the glade, and spotted the broken nest.

"Oh, poor nestie!" he cried. "Who broke it?"

The Fox Twins nudged each other bashfully.

"They didn't do it on purpose," Rupert explained.

"Naughty Foxes!" said Raggety. "But I will fix, with my special nest-building magic!"

"Can I help?" asked Ping Pong.

But Raggety shook his head. "Can't make nests with tricks from books. You need real Raggety Forest Magic!"

The little elf chanted a magic spell. There was a shimmering and a fizzing as a magical wind stirred the twigs. Then. . . nothing.

16

Raggety chanted the spell again, and then he shouted: "Turn leaves and twigs into new nest!"

Sparkles flew from Raggety's hands. But this time they didn't even reach the nest. Instead, they hit the Fox Twins!

"Raggety, what have you done?" cried Rupert.

"Cheep! Cheep!" said the Twins together. The magic had turned them into birds!

Then Rupert had an idea.

"Wait!" he said. "Watch this. Here you are, Freda. Have a nice twig. . ."

He offered Freda a twig. She picked it up in her mouth, then placed it next to the eggs.

Everyone watched in amazement as the Fox Twins – now the Bird Twins – got stuck into rebuilding the nest.

Just as the Twins finished building the nest, the two eggs began to shudder.

"The eggs are nearly hatching!" cried Ping Pong. She and Rupert turned anxiously to Raggety for help.

"Quick, Raggety," Rupert urged. "You must do some nest-lifting magic."

But Raggety didn't know the right spell.

"Do you know nest-lifting magic, Ping Pong?" Raggety asked shyly.

"No," said Ping Pong. Then her eyes widened with excitement. "But mum taught me a flying spell last week. That might work!"

"Brilliant!" said Rupert. "Come on, before they hatch."

24

Ping Pong rubbed some magic powder on her hands. It began to sparkle as she chanted a spell.

Everyone leant forward to watch. For a moment, nothing happened. Then the nest began to rise from the ground.

"Oooh! Aaah!" chorused everyone – except the Bird Twins, who chirruped!

The nest came safely to rest in the tree. The baby birds were going to be all right.

Suddenly, there was another little burst of sparkles and the Bird Twins turned back into the Fox Twins.

"What's going on?" they both asked. "Who rebuilt that nest?"

Rupert had to tell them everything that had happened. Weren't they surprised!

Everyone congratulated Ping Pong – except for Raggety, who looked a bit sad.

"Cheer up," said Ping Pong. "There wouldn't have been a new nest without your magic!"

That made Raggety feel a lot better. He gave Ping Pong a big hug.

Then Rupert heard something overhead. "Listen! He cried. The eggs have hatched."

Everyone looked up, and saw the baby birds sitting in the nest with their mother.

"They sound nearly as lovely as you did!" said Ping Pong to the embarrassed foxes.

"Hmph," said Freda. "I think we've done enough birdy things for one day. Let's go, Freddy."

At that moment, the empty shells fell out of the nest.

Turn over to see where they landed!

The End

First published in Great Britain in 2007
by Egmont UK Limited
239 Kensington High Street, London W8 6SA

ISBN 978 1 4052 3196 1
1 3 5 7 9 10 8 6 4 2
Printed in China